WRITING

MARGUERITE DURAS

translated from the French by

MARK POLIZZOTTI

Lumen Editions
a division of Brookline Books

The Publisher would like to thank the French Ministry of Foreign Affairs for their generosity in making this translation possible.

ISBN 1-57129-053-2

Library of Congress Cataloging-In-Publication Data
Duras, Marguerite.
    [Ecrire. English.]
    Writing / Marguerite Duras ; translated from the French by Mark Polizzotti.
        p. cm.
    ISBN 1-57129-053-2 (pbk.)
    1. Duras, Marguerite--Translations into English.   I. Polizzotti, Mark.   II. Title.
    PQ2607.U8245A27 1998
    844'.912--dc21   98-21440
                                                                                                    CIP

Book design and typography by Erica L. Schultz.

Printed in USA by Edwards Brothers.
10 9 8 7 6 5 4 3 2 1

Published by
Lumen Editions
a division of Brookline Books
P.O. Box 1047
Cambridge, Massachusetts 02238
Order toll-free: 1-800-666-BOOK

Contents

ℭ

ぱ

I called the event that happened in Vauville "The Death of the Young British Pilot." I first told it to Benoît Jacquot, who had come to see me in Trouville. It was his idea to film me talking about the death of that young pilot, who was twenty years old. And so a film was made by Benoît Jacquot. The visuals were by Caroline Champetier de Ribes, and the sound by Michel Vionnet. The setting was my apartment in Paris.

Once the film was completed, we went to my house in Neauphle-le-Château. I talked about writing. I wanted to try to talk about that: Writing. And so a second film was made, using the same crew and produced by the same company (Sylvie Blum and Claude Guisard of I.N.A.).

The text called "Roma" was initially a film entitled "Dialogue in Rome," financed by Italian national television (R.A.I.) at the request of my friend Giovanella Zanoni.

— M. D.
Paris, June 1993

I dedicate this book to the memory of W. J. Cliffe,
dead at the age of twenty, in Vauville, May 1944,
at an undetermined hour.

WRITING

Writing

ꝶ

IT IS IN A HOUSE that one is alone. Not outside it, but inside.
Outside, in the garden, there are birds and cats. And also,
once, a squirrel, and a ferret. One isn't alone in a garden.
But inside the house, one is so alone that one can lose one's
bearings. Only now do I realize I've been here for ten years.
Alone. To write books that have let me know, and others
know, that I was the writer I am. How did that happen?
And how can one express it? What I *can* say is that the kind
of solitude found in Neauphle was created by me. For me.
And that only in this house am I alone. To write. To write,
not as I had up until then, but to write books still unknown

to me and not yet decided on by me and not decided on by anyone. It was there that I wrote *The Ravishing of Lol Stein* and *The Vice-Consul,* and then others after them. I understood that I was alone with my writing, alone and far away from everything. That might have lasted for ten years; I'm not sure anymore. I've rarely counted the time spent writing, nor time in general. I counted the time spent waiting for Robert Antelme and Marie-Louise, his younger sister. After that I stopped counting.

I wrote *The Ravishing of Lol Stein* and *The Vice-Consul* upstairs, in my room, the one with the blue wardrobes that, sadly, some young masons later ruined. Sometimes I also wrote here, at this table in the living room.

I preserved the solitude of those first books. I carried it with me. I've always carried my writing with me wherever I go. Paris. Trouville. New York. It was in Trouville that I ended the madness of becoming Lola Valerie Stein. It was also in Trouville that the name Yann Andrea Steiner appeared to me with unforgettable clarity. That was one year ago.

The solitude of writing is a solitude without which writing could not be produced, or would crumble, drained bloodless by the search for something else to write. When it loses its blood, its author stops recognizing it. And first and foremost it must never be dictated to a secretary, however capable she may be, nor ever given to a publisher to read at that stage.

The person who writes books must always be enveloped by a separation from others. That is one kind of solitude. It is the solitude of the author, of writing. To begin with, one must ask oneself what the silence surrounding one is—with practically every step one takes in a house, at every moment of the day, in every kind of light, whether light from outside or from lamps lit in daytime. This real, corporeal solitude becomes the inviolable silence of writing. I've never spoken about this to anyone. By the time of my first solitude, I had already discovered that what I had to do was write. I'd already gotten confirmation of this from Raymond Queneau. The only judgment Raymond Queneau ever pronounced was this sentence: "Don't do anything but write."

Writing was the only thing that populated my life and made it magic. I did it. Writing never left me.

My room is not a bed, neither here nor in Paris nor in Trouville. It's a certain window, a certain table, habits of black ink, untraceable marks of black ink, a certain chair. And certain habits that I always maintain, wherever I go, wherever I am, even in places where I don't write, such as hotel rooms—like the habit of keeping whiskey in my luggage in case of insomnia or sudden despair. During that time I had lovers. I was rarely without at least one lover. They got used to the solitude in Neauphle. And its charm sometimes allowed them to write books in turn. I rarely gave those lovers my books to read. Women should not let lovers read the books they write. When I had finished a chapter, I hid it from them. This thing is so true, for me, that I wonder how one can manage elsewhere or otherwise when one is a woman and one has a husband or lover. One must also, in such cases, hide the love of one's husband from lovers. Mine has never been replaced. I know this every day of my life.

This house is the place of solitude. And yet it looks out onto a street, a square, a very old pond, the village schools. When the pond is frozen over, children come to skate and keep me from working. I let the children do as they like. I watch over them. Every woman who has had children watches over those children—disobedient, wild, like all children. But what anxiety: the worst kind, every time. And what love.

One does not find solitude, one creates it. Solitude is created alone. I have created it. Because I decided that *here* was where I should be alone, that I would be alone to write books. It happened this way. I was alone in this house. I shut myself in—of course, I was afraid. And then I began to love it. This house became the house of writing. My books come from this house. From this light as well, and from the garden. From the light reflecting off the pond. It has taken me twenty years to write what I just said.

One can walk from one end of this house to the other. Yes, and one can also come and go. And then there is the garden. In it, there are thousand-year-old trees and trees that are still young. And there are larches, apple trees, a walnut tree, plum trees, a cherry tree. The apricot tree is dead. Outside my room is the fabulous rose bush from *The*

Atlantic Man. A weeping willow. There are also Japanese cherries, and irises. And beneath a window of the music room there is a camellia, which Dionys Mascolo planted for me.

First I furnished this house and then I had it repainted. And then, maybe two years after that, my life with it began. I finished *Lol Stein* here; I wrote the ending here and in Trouville, by the sea. Alone, no, I wasn't alone; there was a man with me at the time. But we didn't speak. As I was writing, we had to avoid talking about books. Men cannot stand a woman who writes. That's a cruel thing for men. It's hard for all of them. Except for Robert A.

Still, in Trouville there was the beach, the sea, the vastness of the sky and sands. That's what solitude was here. It was in Trouville that I stared at the sea until nothing was left. Trouville was the solitude of my entire life. I still have that solitude around me, impregnable. Sometimes I close the doors, shut off the telephone, shut off my voice, don't want anything.

No matter what I say, I will never discover why one writes and how one doesn't write.

Sometimes when I'm here alone, in Neauphle, I recognize objects such as a radiator. I remember that there was a large plank on the radiator and that I often sat there, on that plank, to watch the cars go by.

Here, when I'm alone, I don't play the piano. I play fairly well, but I don't play much because I don't think I can play when I'm alone, when there's no one but me in the house. It's hard to endure. Because it seems to make sense all of a sudden. But only writing makes sense in certain personal cases. Since I manipulate it, practice it. Whereas the piano is a distant object, inaccessible now and (for me) forever. I think that if I had played piano professionally, I would never have written books. But I'm not sure. Actually, I think that's false. I think I would have written books no matter what, even with music running alongside. Unreadable books, but whole nonetheless. As distant from words as the unknown object of an objectless love. Like the love of Christ or of J. S. Bach—the two of them breathtakingly equivalent.

Solitude also means, either death or a book. But first and foremost it means alcohol. It means whiskey. Up until now, I have never, really never been able—or else I'd have to search way back… I have never been able to start a book without finishing it. I have never written a book that wasn't already its own justification while it was being written, no matter what book it was. Everywhere. In every season. And I discovered this passion in Les Yvelines, in this very house. I finally had a house in which I could hide in order to write books. I wanted to live in this house. What for? That's how it began, as a joke. Maybe to write, I told myself; maybe I could. I had already started books that I'd abandoned. I had even forgotten their titles. *The Vice-Consul*? No, I never abandoned that one; I often think of it. I no longer think of *Lol Stein*. No one can know Lol V. Stein, not you and not me. I've never entirely understood what Lacan said about her. I was floored by Lacan, that statement of his: "She must never know that she's writing what she writes, because she would be lost. And that would be a tragedy."

That statement has become a kind of identity principle for me, "permission to speak" in a sense totally alien to women.

Finding yourself in a hole, at the bottom of a hole, in almost total solitude, and discovering that only writing can save you. To be without the slightest subject for a book, the slightest idea for a book, is to find yourself, once again, before a book. A vast emptiness. A possible book. Before nothing. Before something like living, naked writing, like something terrible, terrible to overcome. I believe that the person who writes does not have any ideas for a book, that her hands are empty, her head is empty, and that all she knows of this adventure, this book, is dry, naked writing, without a future, without echo, distant, with only its elementary golden rules: spelling, meaning.

The Vice-Consul is a book in which everywhere people screamed with no voice. I don't like that expression, but when I reread the book that's what I find: something like that. It's true, the Vice-Consul screamed every day ... but from a place kept secret from me. As one might pray each day, he screamed. It's all true: he yelled very loud, and in the Lahore night he would fire on the Shalimar Gardens in order to kill. Kill anyone, but kill. He killed simply to kill. So long as "anyone" was all of India in a state of decomposition. He screamed in his home, his Residence, and when he was alone in the dark night of deserted Calcutta. He's mad, the Vice-Consul, mad with intelligence. Every night he kills Lahore.

I never found him in anyone else, only in the actor who played him, my friend, the wonderful Michael Lonsdale—

for me, even when playing other parts, he's still the Vice-Consul of France in Lahore. He is my friend, my brother.

The Vice-Consul is the one I believe in. The Vice-Consul's scream, "the only true politics," was also recorded here, in Neauphle-le-Château. It was here that he called her, she, here, yes. She, A.-M. S., Anna-Maria Guardi. Delphine Seyrig was She. And everyone in the film wept. They wept freely, without knowing the meaning of their tears, inevitable—real tears, like the tears of the destitute.

In life there comes a moment, and I believe that it's unavoidable, that one cannot escape it, when everything is put in doubt: marriage, friends, especially friends of the couple. Not children. Children are never put in doubt. And this doubt grows around one. This doubt is alone, it is the doubt of solitude. It is born of solitude. We can already speak the word. I believe that most people couldn't stand what I'm saying here, that they'd run away from it. This might be the reason why not everyone is a writer. Yes. That's the difference. That is the truth. No other. Doubt equals writing. So it also equals the writer. And for the writer, everyone writes. We've always known this.

I also think that without this primary doubt, there can be no solitude. No one has ever written in two voices. One can sing in two voices, and make music, and play tennis; but write? No, never. From the start I wrote books that were called political. The first was *Abahn Sabana David,* one of the ones I still hold dearest. I think that's a detail, that a book can be more or less difficult to lead than ordinary life. It's just that difficulty exists. A book is difficult to

MARGUERITE DURAS

lead toward the reader, in the direction of his reading. If I hadn't begun writing, I would have become an incurable alcoholic. It's a practical state in which one can be lost and unable to write anymore… That's when one drinks. As soon as one is lost with nothing left to write, to lose, one writes. So long as the book is there, shouting that it demands to be finished, one keeps writing. One is forced to keep up with it. It's impossible to throw a book out forever before it's completely written—that is, alone and free of you who have written it. It's as horrible as a crime. I don't believe people who say, "I tore up my manuscript, I threw the whole thing out." I don't believe it. Either what was written didn't exist for them, or else it wasn't a book. And when it isn't a book, one always knows it. When it can never be a book, no, *that* one doesn't know. Ever.

I would hide my face when I went to bed. I was afraid of myself. I don't know how and I don't know why. And that was the reason I drank liquor before going to sleep. To forget me, forget myself. It immediately enters your bloodstream, and then you can sleep. Alcoholic solitude is harrowing. The heart—yes, that's right. It suddenly beats very fast.

When I was writing in the house, everything wrote. Writing was everywhere. And sometimes when I saw friends, I hardly recognized them. Several years were spent like that, difficult ones for me, yes, this might have lasted for ten years. And even when close friends came to see me, that, too, was horrible. My friends knew nothing about me: they meant well and they came out of kindness, believing they would do me good. And strangest of all is that I thought nothing of it.

This is what makes writing wild. One returns to a savage state from before life itself. And one can always recognize it: it's the savageness of forests, as ancient as time. It is the fear of everything, distinct and inseparable from life itself. One becomes relentless. One cannot write without bodily strength. One must be stronger than oneself to approach writing; one must be stronger than what one is writing. It's an odd thing—not only writing, the written word, but also the howls of animals in the night, of everyone, of you and me, of dogs. It's the massive, appalling vulgarity of society. Pain is also Christ and Moses and the Pharaohs and all the Jews, and all the Jewish children, and it's also the most violent form of happiness. I still believe that.

I bought this house in Neauphle-le-Château with money from the film rights to my book *The Sea Wall*. It was mine; it was in my name. The purchase came before my writing mania, that volcano. I think this house had a lot to do with it. The house consoled me for all the pain of my childhood. In buying it, I immediately knew I had done something important for myself, something definitive. Something for me alone and for my child, for the first time in my life. And I took care of it. And I cleaned it. I took great "care" of it. Afterward, when I became absorbed in my books, I took less care of it.

Writing goes very far ... All the way to having it over with. Sometimes it's untenable. Everything suddenly takes on meaning with respect to what is written: it's enough to drive you insane. You no longer know the people you know and the ones you don't know you think you've been expecting. No doubt it's simply that I was already, a little more than others, tired of living. It was a state of pain without suffering. I did not try to protect myself from other people, especially people who knew me. I wasn't sad. I was desperate. I had launched into the most difficult task I ever faced: my lover from Lahore, writing his life. Writing *The Vice-Consul*. I must have spent three years on that book. I couldn't talk about it, because the slightest intrusion into the book, the slightest "objective" opinion would have erased everything, of that book. Another kind of writing by me, corrected, would have destroyed the writing of the book and my own knowledge of that book. The illusion one has—entirely correct—of being the only one to have written what one has written, no matter if it's worthless or marvelous. And when I read my reviews, most of the time I responded to the fact that people said *it was like nothing else.* In other words, that it reconnected with the initial solitude of the author. ~phenomenology~

This house, here, in Neauphle: I thought I'd also bought it for my friends, to have them come visit, but I was wrong. I bought it for myself. It's only now that I know it, and say it. Some evenings there were many friends here. The Gallimards came often, as did their wives, and their friends. There were a lot of Gallimards—sometimes maybe fifteen of them. I asked people to come a little early to help me move the tables into one room, so we could all be together. Those evenings I'm talking about were very happy occasions for everyone. The happiest of all. There were always Robert Antelme and Dionys Mascolo and their friends. And my lovers, too, especially Gérard Jarlot, who was seduction itself, and who also became a friend of the Gallimards.

When people were there I was simultaneously less alone and more abandoned. You can approach that solitude only through night. At night, imagine Duras in her bed, sleeping alone in a house forty-four hundred feet square. When I went to the other end of the house, over toward the "little cottage," I feared the space like a trap. I can say that every night I was afraid. And yet, I never lifted a finger to have anyone come live here. Sometimes I went out late at night. I loved those meandering walks with people from the village, friends, residents of Neauphle. We drank. We talked, a lot. We went into a kind of cafeteria huge as a village of several acres. It was packed at three in the morning. The name comes back to me now: Parly II. In those places, too, we were lost. There, the waiters watched like cops over the vast territory of our solitude.

This isn't a country home, here, this house. One couldn't say that. It was a farm at first, with the pond, and then it was the country home of a notary, the great corps of Parisian Notaries.

When they opened the main entrance for me, I saw the garden. It lasted several seconds. No sooner had I walked in than I said, Yes, I would buy the house. I bought it then and there. I paid on the spot, in cash.

Now it has become a house for all seasons. And I have also given it to my son. It belongs to both of us. He is as attached to it as he is to me; I believe that now. He has kept everything of mine in this house. I can still be alone here. I have my table, my bed, my telephone, my paintings, and my books. The screenplays of my films. And my son is very happy when I enter this house. That happiness, my son's, is now the happiness of my life.

A writer is an odd thing. He's a contradiction, and he makes no sense. Writing also means not speaking. Keeping silent. Screaming without sound. A writer is often quite restful; she listens a lot. She doesn't speak much because it's impossible to speak to someone about a book one has written, and especially about a book one is writing. It's impossible. It's the opposite of the cinema, the theater, and other performances. It's the opposite of all kinds of reading. It's the hardest of all. It's the worst. Because a book is the unknown, it's the night, it's closed off, and that's that. It's the book that advances, grows, advances in directions one thought one had explored; that advances toward its own fate and the fate of its author, who is annihilated by its publication: her separation from it, the dream book, like the last-born child, always the best loved.

An open book is also night.

I don't know why, but those words I just said make me cry.

Write all the same, in spite of despair. No: with despair. I don't know what to call that despair. Writing to one side of what precedes writing is always to ruin it. And yet we must accept this: ruining the failure means coming back toward another book, toward another possibility of the same book.

This loss of myself in the house was in no way voluntary. I didn't say, "I'm shut up in here every day of the year." I wasn't, and it would have been false to say so. I went out to run errands, I went to the café. But at the same time I was here. The village and the house are the same thing. And the table by the pond. And the black ink. And the white paper, it's all the same thing. And as for the books— no, suddenly it's never the same thing.

Before me, no one had written in this house. I asked the mayor, my neighbors, the shopkeepers. No. Never. I often phoned Versailles to try to find out the names of the people who had lived in this house. In the list of the inhabitants' last names and their first names and their professions, there were never any writers. Now, all these names could have been the names of writers. All of them. But no. Around here there were only family farms. What I found buried in the ground were German garbage pits. The house had in fact been occupied by German officers. Their garbage pits were holes, holes in the ground. There were a lot of oyster shells, empty cans of expensive foodstuffs, especially foie gras, caviar. And much broken china. We threw all of it out. Except the debris of china, without a doubt Sèvres porcelain: the designs were intact. And the blue was the innocent blue in the eyes of certain of our children.

When a book is finished—a book you have written, I mean—you can no longer say when reading it that this particular book is a book you have written, nor what things were written in it, in what state of despair or happiness, of discovery or failure involving your entire being. Because in the final account, nothing like that can be seen in a book. The writing is uniform in some way, tempered. Nothing more happens in such a book, once it's finished and published. And it rejoins the indecipherable innocence of its coming into the world.

To be alone with the as yet unwritten book is still to be in the primal sleep of humanity. That's it. It also means being alone with the writing that is still lying fallow. It means trying not to die. It means being alone in a shelter during the war. But without prayer, without God, with no thought whatsoever except the insane desire to exterminate the German Nation down to the last Nazi.

Writing has always been done without references, or else it is… It is still as it was on the first day. Savage. Different. Except the people, the characters who circulate in the book:

one never forgets them in one's work and never does the author regret them. No, of that I am certain, no, the writing of a book, writing. It is always the open door to abandonment. There is something suicidal in a writer's solitude. One is alone even in one's own solitude. Always inconceivable. Always dangerous. Yes. The price one pays for having dared go out and scream.

In the house, I always used to write on the second floor; I would never write downstairs. Afterward, on the contrary, I wrote in the large living room on the ground floor, perhaps to feel less alone—I don't really know—and also to see the garden.

There is some of this in the book: its solitude is that of the entire world. It is everywhere, has invaded everything. I still believe in this invasion. Like everyone else. Solitude is the thing without which one does nothing. Without which one stops looking at anything. It's a way of thinking, reasoning, but only with one's own everyday thoughts. There is also some of that in the function of writing, and perhaps first and foremost it means telling oneself every day that one mustn't kill oneself, so long as every day one could kill oneself. That is the writing of a book; it is not solitude. I'm talking about solitude, but I wasn't alone since I had this work to complete, to bring to clarity, this forced labor: writing *The Vice-Consul of France in Lahore.* And it was done and translated into every language in the world, and it was preserved. And in this book the Vice-Consul shot at leprosy, at lepers, at the poor, at dogs, and then he began shooting at Whites, the white governors. He killed everyone but her, she who on the morning of a certain day drowned in the Delta, Lola Valerie Stein, the queen of my childhood and of South Tahla, the wife of the governor of Vinh Long.

That book was the first book of my life. It was in Lahore, and also there, in Cambodia, in the plantations; it was everywhere. *The Vice-Consul* started with a child of fifteen who was pregnant, the little Annamite driven from her mother's house who stayed in that blue gravel pit outside Pursat. I don't remember what happens after that. I remember having difficulty finding that place, the mountains of Pursat, where I had never been. The map was on my desk and I traced the paths taken by beggars and children with broken legs, whose eyes had died, who were thrown away by their mothers and who ate garbage. It was a very difficult book to write. There was no possible plan to express the amplitude of the misery, since nothing remained of the visible events that had caused it. Nothing remained but Hunger and Pain.

There was no link between brutal episodes, so there was never any scheduling. There never has been in my life. Never. Neither in my life nor in my books; not once.

I wrote every morning. But without any kind of schedule. Never. Except for cooking. I knew exactly when to come to make something boil or keep something from burning. And for my books I knew it, too. I swear it. I swear all of it. I have never lied in a book. Nor even in my life. Except to men. Never. And this is because my mother had terrified me with the lie that killed children who lied.

I think that what I blame books for, in general, is that they are not free. One can see it in the writing: they are fabricated, organized, regulated; one could say they conform. A function of the revision that the writer often wants to impose on himself. At that moment, the writer becomes his own cop. By being concerned with good form, in other words the most banal form, the clearest and most inoffensive. There are still dead generations that produce prim books. Even young people: charming books, without extension, without darkness. Without silence. In other words, without a true author. Books for daytime, for whiling away the hours, for traveling. But not books that become embedded in one's thoughts and toll the black mourning for all life, the commonplace of every thought.

I don't know what a book is. No one knows. But we know when there is one. And when there's nothing, one knows it the way one knows one is not yet dead.

Every book, like every writer, has a difficult, unavoidable passage. And one must consciously decide to leave this mistake in the book for it to remain a true book, not a lie. I don't yet know what happens to solitude after that. I can't talk about it yet. What I believe is that the solitude becomes banal; eventually it becomes common, and so much the better.

When I spoke for the first time of the love between Anne-Marie Stretter, the French ambassador's wife in Lahore, and the Vice-Consul, I felt like I had destroyed the book, had removed it from its expectation. But no, not only did it stand up, but it was even the opposite. There are also author's mistakes, things like that which are actually strokes of luck. There is something exhilarating about successful, magnificent mistakes, and even the others, the easy kind, such as the ones that come from childhood; those, too, are often marvelous.

I often find others' books "clean," but often as if they derive from a classicism that takes no chances. *Inevitable* would probably be the word. I don't know.

The great readings of my life, the ones for me alone, are things written by men. It's Michelet. Michelet and again Michelet, to the point of tears. Political texts as well, but less so. It's Saint-Just, Stendhal, and strangely enough it isn't Balzac. The Text of Texts is the Old Testament.

I don't know how I got out of what one might call a fit, the way one might say a fit of hysteria or fit of lethargy, of degradation, like feigned sleep. Solitude was that, too. A kind of writing. And reading was the same as writing.

Certain writers are terrified. They are afraid of writing. What matters in my case, perhaps, is that I was never afraid of that particular fear. I wrote incomprehensible books and they were read. There's one I read recently that I hadn't read in thirty years and that I find magnificent. Its title is *Une vie tranquille* [A Peaceful Life]. I had forgotten everything about it except the last sentence: "No one had seen the man drown but me." It's a book that was written in one go, in the banal and very dark logic of a murder. In that book, one can go further than the book itself, than the murder in the book. One can go who knows where, no doubt toward adoration of the sister, the love story between the sister and brother, still, yes, for all eternity, a dazzling, inconsiderate, punished love.

We are sick with hope, those of us from '68. The hope is the one we placed in the role of the proletariat. And as for us, no law, nothing, no one and no thing, will ever cure us of that hope. I'd like to join the Communist Party again. But at the same time I know I shouldn't. And I'd also like to speak to the Right and insult it with all the force of my rage. Insults are just as strong as writing. It's a form of writing, but addressed to someone. I insulted people in my articles, which can be every bit as satisfying as writing a beautiful poem. I draw a radical distinction between a man of the Left and a man of the Right. Some would say they're the same man. On the Left there was Pierre Bérégovoy, who will never be replaced.* Bérégovoy number one is Mitterand, who isn't like anyone else either.

Personally, I'm like everyone else. I don't believe anyone ever turned around to look at me in the street. I am banality itself. The triumph of banality. Like the old woman in my book *Le Camion* [The Truck].

* Bérégovoy was finance minister, then prime minister under Mitterand. He committed suicide in 1993, when Duras was putting the finishing touches to *Writing*. [Trans.]

Living like that, the way I say I lived, in that solitude, eventually means running certain risks. It's inevitable. As soon as a human being is left alone, she tips into unreason. I believe this: I believe that a person left to her own devices is already stricken by madness, because nothing keeps her from the sudden emergence of her personal delirium.

One is never alone. One is never physically alone. Anywhere. One is always somewhere. One hears noises in the kitchen, noises from the television, or the radio, or the neighboring apartments, throughout the building. Especially when one has never demanded silence, as I always have.

I'd like to tell a story that I first told to Michelle Porte, who had made a film about me. At the time, I was in what we might call a state of *expenditure* in the "little" house that is attached to the main house. I was alone. I was waiting for Michelle Porte in that state of expenditure. I often stay alone like that in calm, empty places. A long time. And it was in that silence, on that day, that I suddenly saw and heard, on the wall, very near me, the final moments in the life of a common fly.

I sat on the ground so as not to frighten it. I didn't move.

I was alone with it in the house. I had never thought about flies before, except probably to curse them. Like you.

I was raised like you to be horrified of that universal calamity, the thing that brought plague and cholera.

I leaned closer to watch it die.

It was trying to get away from the wall; it was in danger of becoming prisoner of the sand and cement that the dampness from the garden made stick to the wall. I watched to see how a fly died. It was long. It struggled against death. The whole thing lasted between ten and fifteen minutes, and then it stopped. Its life must have ended. I stayed where I was to watch some more. The fly remained stuck to the wall as I had seen it, as if sealed to itself.

I was mistaken: it was still alive.

I stayed some more to watch, in hopes that it would start to hope again, to live.

My presence made that death even more horrible. I knew it, and still I remained. To see, see how that death would progressively invade the fly. And also to try to see where that death had come from. From outside, or from the thickness of the wall, or from the ground. What night it came from, from earth or sky, from the nearby forests, or from a nothingness as yet unnamable, perhaps very near, perhaps from me, trying to recreate the path the fly had taken as it passed into eternity.

I don't know the ending. No doubt the fly, at the end of its strength, fell. No doubt its legs came unstuck from the wall. And it fell from the wall. I don't know anything more, except that I left. I told myself, "You are going insane." And I left that place.

When Michelle Porte arrived, I showed her the spot and I told her a fly had died there at three twenty. Michelle Porte started to laugh. She couldn't stop laughing. She was right. I smiled at her to put an end to the story. But no: she kept on laughing. And when I tell you this story, plainly, in all truth, in my truth, it's what I just told you: what took place between the fly and me, which is not yet fit to be laughed at.

The death of a fly is still death. It's death marching toward a certain end of the world, which widens the field of the final sleep. When you see a dog die, or a horse die, you say something, like *poor thing…* But when a fly dies, nothing is said, no one records it, nothing.

Now it is written. This might be the kind of very dark slippage—I don't like that word—that one runs the risk of experiencing. It isn't serious, but it's an event in itself, total, with enormous meaning; with inaccessible meaning and limitless breadth. I thought of the Jews. I hated Germany as I had in the earliest days of the war, with all my body and all my strength. Just as during the war, whenever I met a German in the street I thought of his murder committed by me, invented by me, perfected; of the colossal happiness of a German corpse, killed by me.

It's also good if writing leads to that, to that fly—in its death agony, I mean: to write the horror of writing. The exact moment of death, recorded, already rendered it inaccessible. It conferred an overall importance on it—call it a specific place in the general map of life on Earth.

This precision of the moment at which it died meant that the fly had a secret funeral. Twenty years after its death, the proof of it is here: we're still talking about it.

I had never told anyone about the death of that fly, its duration, its slowness, its atrocious fear, its truth.

The precision of the moment of death relates to coexistence with humans, with colonized populations, with the fabulous mass of strangers in the world, of people alone, of universal solitude. Life is everywhere. From bacteria to elephants. From earth to the divine heavens or to those already dead.

I had never organized anything around the death of that fly. The smooth, white walls, its shroud, were already there, and made its death into a public event, something natural and inevitable. The fly had clearly reached the end of its life. I couldn't keep myself from watching it die. It had stopped moving. There was that, and also knowing that one cannot recount the fly's existence.

That was twenty years ago. I had never talked about that event as I've just done, not even to Michelle Porte. What I also realized—what I saw—was that the fly already *knew* that the icy chill passing through it was death. That was the most terrifying thing. The most unexpected. It knew. And it accepted.

A solitary house doesn't simply exist. It needs time around it, people, histories, "turning points," things like marriage or the death of that fly, death, banal death—the death of one and the many at the same time; planetary, proletarian death. The kind that comes with war, those mountains of wars on Earth.

That day. The one dated by a meeting with my friend Michelle Porte, seen by me alone, that day, at no specific hour, a fly died.

The instant I looked at it, it was suddenly three twenty-something in the afternoon: the noise of its outer wings stopped.

The fly was dead.

That queen. Black and blue.

That one, the one *I* had seen, had died. Slowly. It had struggled up to the last spasm. And then it had succumbed. It lasted maybe five to eight minutes. It had been long. It was a moment of absolute terror. And then death departed toward other skies, other planets, other places.

I wanted to run away, and at the same time I told myself I had to look toward that noise on the ground, just so I could hear, for once, that flare-up of green wood, an ordinary fly dying.

Yes. That's right. The death of that fly has become this displacement of literature. One writes without knowing it. One writes by watching a fly relinquish its life. One has a right to do that.

Michelle Porte went into hysterics when I told her the exact time the fly had died. And now I'm thinking that maybe it wasn't because I had recounted that death so laughably. At the time I lacked the words to express it because I was watching that death, the agony of that black and blue fly.

Solitude always goes hand-in-hand with madness. I know this. One does not see madness. Only sometimes can one sense it. I don't believe it can be otherwise. When one takes everything from oneself, an entire book, one necessarily enters a particular state of solitude that cannot be shared with anyone. One cannot share anything. One must read the book one has written alone, cloistered in that book. There is obviously something religious about this, but one doesn't immediately experience it that way. One can think about it later (as I'm thinking about it now) because of something that might be life, for instance, or a solution to the life of the book, of the word, of shouts, silent screams, the silently terrible screams of everyone in the world.

Around us, everything is writing; that's what we must finally perceive. Everything is writing. The fly on the wall is writing; there is much that it wrote in the light of the large room, refracted by the pond. The fly's writing could fill an entire page. And so this would be a kind of writing. From the moment that it could be, it already is a kind of writing. One day, perhaps, in the centuries to come, one might read this writing; it, too, will be deciphered, translated. And the immensity of an illegible poem will unfurl across the sky.

But even so, somewhere in the world people are writing books. Everyone does it. That's what I believe. I am sure this is the case. That for Maurice Blanchot, for example, this is the case. He has madness spinning around him. That madness, too, is death. Not for Georges Bataille. Why was Bataille preserved from free, mad thought? I couldn't say.

I'd like to say a little more about the story of that fly.

I can still see it, that fly, on the white wall, dying. At first in the sunlight, then in the muted light refracted off the tiled floor.

One could also not write, forget a fly. Only watch it. See how it struggled in its turn, terribly and accounted for, in an unknown sky, made of nothing.

There, that's all.

I'm going to speak of nothing.

Of nothing.

All the houses in Neauphle are lived in: not so constantly in the winter, of course, but still they are lived in. They aren't reserved for summer, as is so often the case. All year long they are open, lived in.

What counts in that house in Neauphle-le-Château are the windows overlooking the garden and the road to Paris in front of the house. The one on which the women in my books pass by.

I slept a lot in the room that became the living room. For a long time I thought a bedroom was too conventional. Only when I started working there did it become indispensable like the other rooms—even the empty ones on the upper floors. The mirror in the living room belonged to the previous owners. They left it for me. I bought the piano immediately after the house, for almost the same price.

Alongside the house, a good hundred years ago, there was a path for the livestock to come drink from the pond. The pond is now in my garden. There are no more livestock. And so the village has no more fresh milk in the morning. For the past hundred years.

When we make a film here, the house looks like that other house, the one it once was for the other people before us. In its solitude, its grace, it suddenly shows itself as another house that might still belong to other people. As if something as monstrous as the loss of this house could even be imagined.

The place inside where we put the fruit, the vegetables, the salted butter to keep them cool… There was a room like that… dark and cool… I believe that's what an *ex-*

penditure is; yes, that's it. That's the word. You stock up for the war by putting things under cover.

The first plants here were the ones on the window sills at the entry. The rose geranium that came from the south of Spain. Pungent like the Orient.

We never throw out flowers in this house. It's a habit, not a rule. Never, not even dead ones; we leave them there. There are some rose petals that have been in a jar for forty years. They are still very pink. Dry and Pink.

The problem all year round is dusk. Summer and winter alike.

There is the first dusk, the summer kind, when you mustn't turn the lights on indoors.

And then there is true dusk, winter dusk. Sometimes we close the shutters just not to see it. There are chairs, too, which we put away for the summer. The porch is where we stay every summer. Where we talk with friends who come during the day. Often simply for that, to talk.

It's sad every time, but not tragic: winter, life, injustice. Absolute horror on a certain morning.
It's only that: sad. One doesn't get used to it with time.

The hardest thing in this house is fear for the trees. Always. Every time. Every time there's a storm (and there are a lot of them here), we are with the trees; we worry about those trees. Suddenly I can't remember their name.

Dusk is the time when everyone around the writer stops working.

In the cities, the villages, everywhere, writers are solitary people. Everywhere, always, they have been.

All over the world, the end of light means the end of work.

As for myself, I've always experienced that time not as the moment when work ends, but when it begins. A sort of reversal of natural values by the writer.

The other kind of work writers do is the kind that sometimes makes them feel ashamed, the kind that usually provokes the most violent political regrets. I know that it leaves one inconsolable. And that one becomes as vicious as the dogs used by their police.

Here, one feels separated from manual labor. But against that, against this feeling one must adapt to, get used to, nothing is effective. What will always predominate—and this can drive us to tears—is the hell and injustice of the working world. The hell of factories, the exaction of the employers' scorn and injustice, the horror they breed, the horror of the capitalist regime, of all the misery stemming from it, of the right of the wealthy to do as they please with the proletariat and to make this the very basis of their failure, never of their success. The mystery is why the proletariat should accept. But there are many of us, more of us each day, who believe that it can't last much longer. That something was attained by all of us, perhaps a new reading of their shameful texts. Yes, that's it.

I won't push the point; I'm leaving. But I'm only saying what everyone feels, even if they don't know how to live it.

Often with the end of work comes the memory of the greatest injustice of all. I'm talking about the ordinariness of life. Not in the morning, only in the evening does this come, even into the houses, to us. And if one isn't that way, then one isn't anything at all. One is nothing. And always, in every case, in every village, this is known.

Deliverance comes when night begins to settle in. When work stops outside. What remains is the luxury we all share, the ability to write about it at night. We can write at any hour of the day. We are not sanctioned by orders, schedules, bosses, weapons, fines, insults, cops, bosses, and bosses. Nor by the brooding hens of tomorrow's fascisms.

The Vice-Consul's struggle is at once naive and revolutionary.

That is the major injustice of time, of all times: and if one doesn't cry about it at least once in life, then one doesn't cry about anything. And never to cry means not to live.

Crying has to happen, too.

Even if it's useless to cry, I still think we have to cry. Because despair is tangible. It remains. The memory of despair remains. Sometimes it kills.

To write.

I can't.

No one can.

We have to admit: we cannot.

And yet we write.

It's the unknown one carries within oneself: writing is what is attained. It's that or nothing.

One can speak of a writing sickness.

What I'm trying to say isn't easy, but I believe we can find our way here, comrades of the world.

There is a madness of writing that is in oneself, an insanity of writing, but that alone doesn't make one insane. On the contrary.

Writing is the unknown. Before writing one knows nothing of what one is about to write. And in total lucidity.

It's the unknown in oneself, one's head, one's body. Writing is not even a reflection, but a kind of faculty one has, that exists to one side of oneself, parallel to oneself: another person who appears and comes forward, invisible, gifted with thought and anger, and who sometimes, through his own actions, risks losing his life.

If one had any idea what one was going to write, before doing it, before writing, one would never write. It wouldn't be worth it anymore.

Writing is trying to know beforehand what one would write if one wrote, which one never knows until afterward; that is the most dangerous question one could ever ask oneself. But it's also the most widespread.

Writing comes like the wind. It's naked, it's made of ink, it's the thing written, and it passes like nothing else passes in life, nothing more, except life itself.

The Death of
the Young British Pilot

ℭ

THE BEGINNING, the opening of a story.

It's a story I'm going to tell for the first time. The story of this book.

I believe it's a direction that writing takes. That's it— this writing addressed to you, for instance, about whom I know nothing yet.

To you, reader:

It takes place in a village very near Deauville, a few miles from the sea. The village is called Vauville. In the *département* of Calvados.

Vauville.
It's there. It's the name on the road sign.

When I went there for the first time, it was on the advice of friends, shopkeepers in Trouville. They had told me of the lovely chapel in Vauville. And so I saw the church that day, that first time, without seeing anything of what I'm about to relate.

The church is in fact quite beautiful, even lovely. To its right is a small cemetery from the nineteenth century, noble, opulent, reminiscent of Père-Lachaise in Paris, very ornate, like an immobile celebration, frozen in the middle of the centuries.

On the other side of the church is the body of the young British pilot killed on the last day of the war.

And in the middle of the lawn, there is a grave. A light grey granite slab, perfectly polished. I didn't see that stone right away. I saw it after I learned the story.

He was an English child.

He was twenty years old.

His name is engraved on the slab.

At first they called him the Young British Pilot.

He was an orphan. He was in a boarding school in the suburbs north of London. He had enlisted like so many young Englishmen.

It was in the last days of the world war. Perhaps *the* last: it's possible. He had attacked a German battery. For fun. Since he had fired on their battery, the Germans responded. They fired on the child. He was twenty years old.

The child remained a prisoner of his airplane. A single-seat Meteor.

Yes, that's right. He remained a prisoner of the airplane. And the plane fell onto a tree in the forest. It was there—or so the villagers believe—that he died, during the night, the last of his life.

For a whole day and night, in the forest, all the inhabitants of Vauville kept vigil over him. As before, in ancient times, as they would have done before, they kept vigil with candles, prayers, songs, tears, flowers. And then they managed to pry him out of the plane. And they pried the plane out of the tree. It was long and difficult. His body had remained prisoner of the twisted steel and the tree.

They brought him down from the tree. It was very long. By the end of the night, it was done. Once the body was down, they carried it to the cemetery and immediately dug his grave. And the next day, I believe, they bought the light grey granite slab.

That is the beginning of the story.

The young Englishman is still there, in that grave. Under the granite slab.

The year after his death, someone came to see the young British soldier. He had brought flowers. An old man, also British. He came there to cry over the child's grave and to pray. He said he'd been the child's teacher in a boarding school north of London. It was he who spoke the child's name.

It was also he who said the child was an orphan. That there was no one to notify.

Every year he came back. For eight years.
And beneath the granite slab, death lingered on and on.

And then he never came back again.

And no one was left on Earth to remember the existence of that wild child—crazy, some said: that crazy child, who had won the world war single-handedly.

Then there were only the villagers to remember and tend the grave, the flowers, the grey stone slab. I think that for years no one knew the story, apart from the people of Vauville.

The teacher had spoken the child's name. His name was engraved on the tomb:

W. J. Cliffe.

Every time the old man talked about the child, he wept.

On the eighth year, he did not come back. And he never came back again.

My younger brother had died during the war with Japan. He died without any grave at all. Thrown into a mass pit on top of the previous corpses. And this is something so terrible to think about, so horrible, that it cannot be endured, and one cannot know just how horrible without having lived through it. It's not the heap of bodies, not at all; it's the disappearance of that body in the mass of other bodies. It's his, his own body, thrown into the trench, without a word. Except a prayer for all the dead.

It wasn't the same for the young British pilot, since the villagers had sung and prayed on their knees on the ground around his tomb and stayed there all night. Even so, it brought me back to that mass grave on the outskirts of Saigon where Paulo's body lies. But now I think there's more than that. I believe that one day, much later, and later still, I don't know for sure, but I already know, yes, much later, I will find—I already know this—something material that I will recognize as a smile frozen in the sockets of his eyes. Paulo's eyes. Here, there's more than Paulo. For the death of that young British pilot to become such a personal event, there is more to it than I believe.

I will never know what. No one will ever know.
No one.

It brings me back to our love as well. There is the love of
one's little brother and there was our love, ours, his and
mine, very strong love, hidden, culpable, a love for every
moment. Still lovely even after your death. The young English corpse was everyone and it was also he alone. It was
everyone and he. But "everyone" does not make you cry.
And then the desire to see the dead child, to verify without
ever having known him if that had indeed been his face,
that hole at the end of his eyeless body; that desire to see
his body and how his face looked in death, ripped apart by
the steel of the Meteor.

Could any of it still be seen? The thought is almost unbearable. I never thought I could write it. That was my
business, not the reader's. You are my reader, Paulo. Because I'm telling you, I'm writing it to you, it's true. You are
the love of my entire life, the keeper of our rage against our
older brother, throughout our childhood, your childhood.

The grave stands alone. As he was alone. It has its age of
death ... how can I say it ... no one knows ... the state of
the lawn, the little garden. The proximity of the other cemetery was also part of it. But honestly, how can I say that?
How can one bring together the infant who was six months
old when he died and whose grave is in the upper part of
the lawn, and that other child who was twenty? They are
still there, both of them, and their names, and their ages.
They are alone.

And afterward I saw other things. Always, afterward, one sees things.

I saw the sky and sunlight streaming through the trees; mutilated, black trees, also killed in the fields. I saw that the trees were still black. And then there was also the village school. And I heard children singing "I'll never forget you." For you. Alone. At the origin of all this there was now that someone, and that child, my child, and my little brother, and someone else, the English child. The same. Death baptizes as well.

Here, we are far removed from identity. He's a corpse, a twenty-year-old corpse who will go on to the end of time. That's all. His name is no longer worth telling: he was a child.

That's all we need to know.

We can remain here, at this particular point in the life of a twenty-year-old child, the last man to die in the war.

Any death is still Death. Any child of twenty is a child of twenty.

It's not entirely the death of just anyone. It remains the death of a child.

Anyone's death is Death in its entirety. Anyone is everyone. And this anyone can take the horrible form of an ongoing childhood. They know these things in villages; the peasants taught them to me with the brutality of an event that became *that* event, of a child of twenty killed in a war at which he was playing.

Perhaps that is also why he remained intact, the young English corpse; why he remained stuck in that terrible, horrible age, the age of twenty.

I became friendly with the people of the village, especially the old woman who looks after the church.

The dead trees are there, crazy, frozen in their fixed chaos; the wind wants no part of them. They are complete, martyred, black with the dark blood of trees killed by fire.

He became sacred for me—me, the passer-by—he, the young Englishman who died at twenty. Each time I wept for him.

And then I regretted not having known the old English gentleman who came every year to shed tears over the child's grave, not having talked to him about the child, about his laugh, his eyes, his games.

The dead child was taken in charge by the entire village. And the village adored him. This child of war will forever have flowers on his grave. One thing remains unknown: the exact date when it all stopped.

In Vauville, the memory of the beggar woman's song comes back to me. That very simple song. The song of the insane, of all the insane, everywhere; those who went insane from indifference. The song of easy death. Of those who died of hunger. The memory of those who died on the road, in the trenches, half devoured by dogs, tigers, birds of prey, giant rats from the marshes.

The hardest thing to endure is the destroyed face, the skin, the sunken eyes. Eyes emptied of sight, with no more gaze. Staring. Looking toward nothing.

He is twenty years old. The age, the number of his age stopped at death; what he has become will always be twenty years old. No one knows what that is. No one looked.

I wanted to write about the English child. And I can't write about him anymore. And yet I'm writing, as you see, I'm writing nonetheless. It's because I'm writing that I don't know if it can be written about. I know it isn't a story. It's a brutal, isolated fact, without reverberation. The facts suffice. One could relate the facts. And the old man who always cried, who came for eight years, and who, one particular time, did not come back. Ever. Was he, too, taken by death? Without a doubt. And then the story would end for all eternity, like the child's blood, his eyes, the child's smile frozen by the discolored mouth of death.

The children in school sing that they had loved him for a long time, that child of twenty, and that they'd never forget him. They sing it every afternoon.

And I weep.

There were nightfalls of the same blue as the eyes of those schoolchildren.

There was that color blue in the sky, the blue which was the color of the sea. There were all the trees that had been assassinated. And the sky, too. I looked at it. It covered everything with its slowness, its everyday indifference. Unfathomable.

I see places linked together. Except the continuity of the forest: that has disappeared.

Suddenly I no longer wanted to go back. And still I wept.

I saw him everywhere, the dead child. The child who had died from playing at war, from playing at being the wind, at being a twenty-year-old Englishman, handsome and heroic. Who played at being happy.

I still see you: you. The Child himself. Dead like a bird, of eternal death. Death that was long in coming. In the pain of his body ripped apart by airplane steel, he begged God to let him die quickly so that he wouldn't suffer anymore.

His name was W. J. Cliffe, yes. That's what is now inscribed on the grey granite.

You have to cross the churchyard and head toward the town school, which stands in the same enclosure. Go toward the cats, those crazy gangs of cats, with their cruel and incredible beauty. Those cats called "tortoiseshell," yellow like flames, red like blood, white and black. Black like the trees forever blackened by the soot of German bombs.

A river runs along the cemetery. And then in the distance are more dead trees, to the other side of where the child is. Burnt trees that scream against the direction of the wind. It's a very loud sound, like a strident sweeping of the end of the world. It makes you afraid. And then, suddenly, it stops, without your knowing what it was. For no reason, you'd say, for no reason at all. And then the peasants say it was nothing, just the trees that have preserved in their sap the charcoal of their wounds.

The inside of the church is truly admirable. One can recognize everything. The flowers are flowers, the plants, the colors, the altars, the embroideries, the tapestries. It's admirable. Like a temporarily abandoned room awaiting lovers who haven't arrived yet because of bad weather.

One would like to get somewhere with that emotion. Write from without, perhaps, by simply describing, perhaps, describing the things there, present. Not invent any others. Invent nothing, no detail. Not invent anything at all. Nothing like anything. Not accompany death. To finally leave it behind and not look in that direction, just for once.

The roads that lead to the village are former paths, and very old. They come from prehistory. They have always been there, it seems; that's what I'm told. They were the necessary passageways toward the terra incognita of footpaths and springs and seashores, or if one wanted to be safe from wolves.

I had never been devastated by the fact of death to such a point. Utterly captured. Caught. And now, for me, all those surroundings are finished; I don't go there anymore.

What remains is Vauville, that hopscotch; what remains is deciphering the names on certain tombs.

What remains is the forest, the forest that moves closer to the sea with each passing year. Still black with soot, ready for the coming eternity.

The dead child was also a soldier in the war. And he could just as well have been a French soldier. Or an American.

We are eleven miles from the landing beach.

The villagers knew he was from the north of England. The old English gentleman had told them about the child. The old man wasn't the child's father, the child was an orphan; he must have been his teacher, or perhaps a friend of his parents. The man loved that child. Like his own son. Like a lover, too, perhaps, who knows? He was the one who had spoken the child's name. The name was engraved on the light grey slab. W. J. Cliffe.

There is nothing I can say.

There is nothing I can write.

There should be a writing of non-writing. Someday it will come. A brief writing, without grammar, a writing of words alone. Words without supporting grammar. Lost. Written, there. And immediately left behind.

I'd like to tell of the ceremony that was created around the death of the young British pilot. I know a few details: the whole village was involved; it recaptured an almost revolutionary initiative. I also know that the tomb was erected without official authorization. That the mayor had no part in it. That Vauville became a kind of funeral celebration centered on the adoration of the child. A celebration free of tears and love songs.

All the villagers know the child's story. And also the story of the old man's visits, the old teacher. But they never talk about the war anymore. For them, the war was only that child killed at the age of twenty.

Death had reigned over the village.

The women cried, they couldn't help it. The young pilot disappears; he dies a real death. If they sang his death, for example, it wouldn't be the same story. The sublime discretion of those women, who saw to it, I believe (though I can't be completely sure), that the child was put on the other side of the church, where there were no other graves yet. Where there is still only his grave. Sheltered from the crazy wind. The women took the child's body, they washed the body, and they put it in that place, in the grave, the one with the pale grey slab.

The women never said anything about that. If I had been there with them, to do it with them, I wouldn't have been able to write about it; I don't believe so. I'm saying that this incredibly strong feeling of involvement might not have occurred. It's the same emotion that still returns today, when I'm alone. Alone, I still cry for the child who became the war's final casualty.

That inexhaustible fact: the death of a twenty-year-old child killed by German guns on the very day peace was declared.

Twenty years old. I'm saying his age. I'm saying: he was twenty years old. He will be twenty years old for eternity, before the Eternal. Whether he exists or not, the Eternal will be that child.

When I say twenty years old, it's horrible. His age is the most horrible thing. The pain I feel for him is a banality. It's odd, but the idea of God never occurred around the child. That easy word, the word *God,* the easiest of all—no one spoke it. It was never uttered during the burial of the twenty-year-old child, who had been playing at war in his Meteor above the Norman forest, beautiful as the sea.

Nothing measures up to this fact. There are many facts like this in the universe. Breaches. There, this event was seen. And the fact that the child died from playing at war was seen, too. Everything surrounding the child's death is clear.

He had been happy, he had been very happy coming out of the forest; he didn't see any Germans. He was happy to fly, to live, to have decided to kill some German soldiers. Like all children, this child loved to play war. Dead, he was always another child, any twenty-year-old child. And then it stopped with the night, the first night. He became the child of this French village, he, the British pilot.

He signed his death here, before the people of Vauville who were watching.

This book is not a book.

It's not a song.

Nor a poem. Nor thoughts.

But tears, pain, crying, despair that cannot yet be stopped nor reasoned with. Political fury strong like one's faith in God. Even stronger than that. More dangerous because it is endless.

That child who died in the war is also the secret of each one who found him at the top of that tall tree, crucified on that tree by the carcass of his airplane.

One cannot write about that. Or else one can write about everything. To write about everything, everything at once, is not writing. It's nothing. To read it is untenable, like reading an advertisement.

Again I hear the singing of the small children from the village school. The singing of the children of Vauville. We should be able to stand it. It's still difficult for us. I always cried when I heard those children singing. And I still cry.

Already one sees the tomb of the young British pilot less. It remains visible in the surrounding landscape, but already it has moved away from us for all eternity. And its eternity will be lived in that way through the lost child.

The places around the church are what give access to the child's grave. There, something is still going on. We are now separated from the event by decades, and yet it's here, the event of his grave is here. Could it be the solitude of a child who died in the war, of gentle caresses on the icy granite of his tombstone? We don't know.

The village has become the village of that twenty-year-old British child. It is like a kind of purity, an abundance of tears. The extreme care taken over his grave will be eternal. We already know this.

The eternity of the young British child-pilot is there, present; one can kiss the grey stone, touch it, sleep against it, weep.

Like an appeal, that word—*eternity* comes to one's lips—will be the common grave of all the other casualties of the region killed in all the wars to come.

This might be the birth of a cult. Replacing God? No, God is replaced every day. One is never short of God.

I don't know what to call this story.

Everything is there, contained in a few dozen square yards. Everything is there in that jumble of dead bodies, the splendor of the tombs, the opulence that make this place so striking. It's not numbers: numbers have been scattered elsewhere, in the German fields of northern Germany, in the slaughters of every region of the Atlantic coastline. The child has always remained himself. And alone. Battlefields have always been far away, everywhere in Europe. Here it's the opposite. Here it's the child, the king of wartime death.

He's a king as well: a child as alone in death as a king in the same death.

One could photograph the tomb. The fact of the tomb. Of the name. Of the sunsets. The sooty blackness of the scorched trees. Photograph those twin rivers gone mad that scream every evening, we'll never know why or at what, like starving bitches; those badly made rivers, God's failures, ill born, that slam together every night, hurl themselves at each other. I've never seen that anywhere else. Madwomen from another world, in a screech of iron, butchery, and convoys, looking for a place to throw themselves, into some sea, into some forest. And the cats, the hordes of cats yowl in terror. There are always cats in cemeteries that lie in wait for who knows what event, indecipherable except to them, the cats. Without owners. Lost.

The dead trees, the fields, the cattle, everything here looks toward the evening sun of Vauville.

The place itself remains absolutely deserted. Empty, yes. Almost empty.

The church caretaker lives right nearby. Every morning after coffee, she goes to look at the grave. A peasant. She wears the same dark blue canvas apron that my mother wore in the Pas-de-Calais, when she was twenty.

I forgot: there is also the new cemetery, less than a mile out of Vauville. It's a five-and-ten-cent cemetery. There are sprays of flowers big as trees. Everything is painted white. And no one is there, no one is inside, you'd think that there wasn't anything. That it isn't a cemetery. That it is I don't know what—a golf course, perhaps.

All around Vauville are very old roads from before the Middle Ages. It was on them that they built roads for us today. Along the ancient hedges, there are new roads for the living. Robert Gallimard was the one who told me about the existence of that whole network of early Norman roads. The first roads of the men of the coast, the North-men.

No doubt many people have written the history of the roads.

What must be said here is the impossibility of telling about this place, here, and this grave. But even so, one can kiss the grey granite and weep over you. W. J. Cliffe.

We must start backward. I'm not talking about writing. I'm talking about the book once it's written. Start at the source and follow it to its water supply. Start from the grave and follow it to him, the young British pilot.

There are often narratives but very seldom writing.

There is only a poem, perhaps, and even then, to try ... what? We no longer know, not even that, what must be done.

There is the grandiose banality of the forest, of the poor, of the mad rivers, the dead trees, and those cats, carnivorous as dogs. Those red and black cats.

The innocence of life, yes, it's true, it is there, like the rounds the schoolchildren sing.

It's true, there is the innocence of life.

An innocence to cry for. In the distance there is the old war, the one that now lies in shreds when one stands alone in the village, facing the martyred trees burnt to cinders by German fire. The corpses of soot trees, assassinated. No. There is no more war. The child has replaced everything of that war. The twenty-year-old child. The entire forest, the entire earth: he replaced it all, along with the future of war. War is locked up in his grave with the bones of the child's body.

It's calm now. The main splendor is the idea, the idea of twenty years old, the idea of playing at war, grown resplendent. A crystal.

If there weren't things like this, writing would never take place. But even if writing is there, always ready to scream, to cry, one does not write it. Emotions of that order, very subtle, very profound, very carnal, and essential, and completely unpredictable, can hatch entire lives in a body. That's what writing is. It's the pace of the written word passing through your body. Crossing it. That's where one starts to talk about those emotions that are hard to say, that are so foreign, and yet that suddenly grab hold of you.

I was at home in this village, here, in Vauville. I came here every day to cry. And then one day I stopped coming.

I write because of the good fortune I have to get mixed up in everything, with everything; the good fortune to be in this battlefield, in this theater devoid of war, in the enlargement of this reflection. And there in the enlargement that slowly, very slowly, gains on the terrain of war, is the ongoing nightmare of the death of that young child of twenty, in the dead body of the English child twenty years of age, dead with the trees of the Norman forest, in the same death, unlimited.

This emotion will continue to spread beyond itself, toward the infinity of the whole world. For centuries. And then one day, all over the world we will understand something like love. Of him. Of the English child who died at twenty for having played at war against the Germans in that monumental forest—so beautiful, they'll say, so ancient, secular, even lovely, yes, that's it: *lovely* is the word.

One should be able to make a certain film. A film of insistence, of flashbacks, new beginnings. And then abandon it. And also film that abandonment. But no one will do it, we already know this. No one will ever do it.

Why not make a film about what is unknown, still unknown?

I have nothing in hand, nothing in mind for making that film. But it's the one I thought about most that summer. Because this film would be the film of the mad, unattainable idea, a film about the literature of living death.

The writing of literature is what poses a problem to every book, to every writer, to every writer's every book. And without that writing there is no writer, no book, nothing. From there, it seems one can also tell oneself that because of this fact, there is perhaps nothing more.

The silent collapse of the world might have begun that day, with the event of the so slow and so painful death of the twenty-year-old Englishman in the sky over the Norman forest, that monument of the Atlantic coast, that glory. That news, that single fact, that mysterious news had infiltrated the heads of those who were still alive; a point of no return had been reached in the primary silence of the earth. From then on they knew it was pointless to keep hoping. They knew it all over the world, starting from that one object, a twenty-year-old child, that young casualty of the last war, the forgotten one from the final war of the first era.

And then one day, there will be nothing left to write, nothing to read, nothing left but the untranslatable fact of the life of that dead boy who was so young, young enough to make you scream.

Roma

ॐ

ITALY.

Rome.

A hotel lobby.

Evening.

The Piazza Navona.

The lobby is empty except for the terrace, a woman sitting in an armchair.

Waiters carry trays; they're going to serve the guests on the terrace. They return, disappear toward the far end of the lobby. Return.

The woman has fallen asleep.

A man arrives. He's also a guest at the hotel. He stops. He looks at the sleeping woman.

He sits down, stops looking at her.

The woman awakes.

The man speaks to her, timidly:

"Am I disturbing you?"

The woman gives him a slight smile; she doesn't answer.

"I'm a guest at the hotel. I see you cross the lobby every day and sit there." (Pause.) "Sometimes you fall asleep. And I watch you. And you know it."

Silence. She looks at him. They look at each other. She says nothing. He asks:

"Have you finished shooting?"
"… Yes …"

"So the script was complete ... ?"

"Yes, we already had one. I wrote it before we started filming."

They don't look at each other. Their discomfort becomes visible. He murmurs:

"The film would begin here, now, at this moment ... when the light fades."

"No. The film already began here, with your question about the shooting."

Pause. Their discomfort increases.

"How's that?"

"With just your question about the shooting, here, a moment ago, the old film disappeared from my life."

Pause—slowness.

"Afterward ... you don't know ..."

"No ... nothing ... Nor do you ..."

"It's true. Nothing."

"And you?"

"I didn't know anything before this moment."

They turn toward the Piazza Navona. She says:

"I never knew. They filmed the fountains on April 27, 1982, at eleven in the evening ... You weren't at the hotel yet."

They gaze at the fountain.

"It looks like it rained."
"It seems that way every night. But it isn't raining. It hasn't been raining in Rome these past days ... It's the water from the fountains that the wind blows onto the ground. The entire square is drenched."
"The children are barefoot ..."
"I watch them every evening."

Pause.

"It's getting chilly."
"Rome is very near the sea. That chill comes from the sea. You already knew that."
"Yes, I think so."

Pause.

"There are guitars, too ... aren't there? It sounds like they're singing..."
"Yes, with the noise of the fountains ... everything blends together. But they are singing."

They don't listen.

"It would all have been false ..."
"I'm not sure ... Maybe nothing would have been. We have no way of knowing ..."
"Is it already too late?"
"Perhaps. Too late even before the start."

Silence. She goes on:

"Look at the large central fountain. It looks frozen, pallid."

"I was looking at it … It's under electric light. You'd think there was a flame inside the cold water."

"Yes. What you see in those furrows in the stone are the flow of other rivers. Rivers from the Middle East and much farther away, from Central Europe; the course of their flow."

"And those shadows on the people."

"Those are the shadows of other people, who are looking at the river."

A long pause. She says:

"I'm afraid that Rome existed …"

"Rome existed."

"Are you sure …"

"Yes, and the rivers, too. And the rest as well."

"How can you stand that …"

Silence. She says in a whisper:

"I don't know what this fear is, other than what one sees in the eyes of those women in the stelae on Via Appia. One sees only what they show of themselves, what they conceal when they show themselves to us. Where are they leading us, toward what night? Even that illusion of clarity reflected off the white stones, perfect, regular—we still doubt it, don't we?"

"You seem to fear the visible side of things."

"I'm afraid as if I were suffering from Rome itself."

"From perfection?"

"No … from its crimes."

A long pause. Glances. Then they lower their eyes.

He says:

"What is that constant thought that makes you so pale, that sometimes makes you shut yourself away on this terrace, waiting for daylight …"

"You knew I couldn't sleep."

"Yes. I couldn't sleep, either. Like you."

"Already, you see."

A pause.

"What is that distraction you're caught up in?"

"I'm constantly finding myself turned away from Rome by a philosophy other than its own … which would have been contemporaneous with Rome's, and which originated somewhere other than here, far from here, from Rome, in the direction of northern Europe, for example, you see …"

"By a philosophy that has left nothing behind?"

"Nothing but a kind of vague memory—invented, perhaps, but plausible."

"It was in Rome that you remembered that northern country."

"Yes. How do you know?"

"I don't know."

"Yes. It was here, in Rome, in the school bus."

A pause. Silence.

"Sometimes in the evening, around sunset, the colors of Via Appia are those of Tuscany. I learned of that northern region when I was very young, still a child. First in a travel guidebook. And then during a school trip. It was a civilization contemporary with Rome that has now disappeared. I wish I knew how to tell you about the beauty of that region, where that civilization and that philosophy occurred in a lovely and fleeting coincidence. I wish I could tell you about the simplicity of their existence, their geography, the color of their eyes, of their climates, their agriculture, their pastures, their skies." (A pause.) "You see, it would be like your smile, but lost, untraceable after it occurs. Like your body, but vanished; like a love, but without you or me. And so how can one say? How can one not love?"

Silence. Delayed glances.

A pause. They are silent. He looks toward the distance, toward nothing. She says:

"I do not believe that Rome had a philosophy, you see. It enunciated its power. People philosophized somewhere else, in those other regions. It was somewhere else that philosophy occurred. Rome was to be only the place of war, the place where that philosophy was stolen and where it was decreed."

"At first, what did that guidebook and that trip tell you?"

"The book said that everywhere else one could find works of art, statuary, temples, civic buildings, public baths, red-light districts, arenas for executions—and that there, in those moors, nothing like that could be found.

"I read that in childhood. Then it was forgotten.

"And then another time there was a ride in the school bus and the teacher said that this civilization had existed there in a splendor never reached anywhere else, in the region the bus was driving through.

"It was raining that afternoon. There was nothing to see. So the teacher spoke about the moors of heather and ice. And we listened to her as we might have looked at her. As we might have looked at those moors ..."

Silence. He asks:

"The region was flat, without contour, and you couldn't see anything?"

"Nothing. Except the line of the sea at the far end of the fields. None of us had ever thought about the moor—never, you understand ... Not yet."

"And Rome?"

"Rome was taught in school."

"The teacher spoke ..."

"Yes. The teacher said that—although we couldn't see anything—a civilization had been created there. In that place on earth. And that it must have been there still, buried under the plain."

"The infinite plain."

"Yes. It ended at the sky. Nothing remained of that civilization: only holes, cavities in the earth, invisible from outside. We asked: Did they know those holes weren't graves? No, she answered, but we've never known if they weren't temples. All we knew is that they had been made, built by human hands.

"The teacher said that sometimes those holes were as large as bedrooms, sometimes large as palaces, that sometimes they became like hallways, passageways, hidden developments. That all these things had been made by human hands, built by them. That in certain deep layers of clay, they had found traces of those hands flattened against the walls. The hands of men, open, sometimes injured."

"What did the teacher think those hands were?"

"They were screams, she said, for later on, for other men to hear and see. Screams made with hands."

"How old were you when you took that trip?"

"I was twelve and a half. I was awestruck. Beneath the sky, above the holes, we could still see cultures that had reached year after year down through the centuries all the way to us, the little girls in the school bus."

Silence. She looks. Recognizes.

"The holes are very near the ocean. They follow the sand embankments, in the arable soil of the moor. The moor crosses through no village. The forest has vanished. After its disappearance, the moor was not renamed. No. It has been there in space and time since it emerged from the central mud of the submerged earth. This is known. But we can no longer see or touch it. It's finished."

"How do we know what you're telling me?"

"How we know this, we will never know … We know. Probably because we have always known it, we have always asked the question and people have always answered the same way. This has been so for thousands of years. They tell it to every child at the age of reason, they teach the facts: 'Look, those holes you see were made by men who came from the North.'"

"As elsewhere they say: 'Look at the flat stones of Jerusalem. That's where mothers rested on the day before their sons were crucified, those fanatics of the God of Judea whom Rome branded criminals.'"

"The same way. They say: 'Look, there, in the same way, the sunken lane was for going to fetch water, and also for traveling from the country to the merchants in the city, and also for the thieves of Jerusalem to go to Calvary to be hanged. It was the only road for all those things. And it was also for children to play in.'"

Silence.

"Can we also talk here about a celebrated love?"
"I'm not sure... Yes, no doubt..."

Silence. Discomfort. Altered voices.

"Who could she have been, the woman in that love story?"
"I would say, for example, a queen of the deserts. In official history, that's what she was: the Queen of Samaria."
"And the man who won the Samaritan war, the one who would have answered?"
"A general in the Roman legions. The head of the Empire."
"I believe you're right."

Silence. Heavier, as if far away.

"All of Rome knew the story of that war."

"Yes. Rome knew history only through wars. And here the difficulties love encountered were linked to the publicity that surrounded the war out of love for her, the Queen of Samaria."

"Yes. That love was great. How did they know?"

"In the same way they knew the number of the dead, the number spoken in low voices at night; they knew the number of prisoners. In peacetime they would have known just the same. Because he made her a captive instead of putting her to death, they would have known it just the same."

"Yes."

"In the midst of those thousands of deaths, that young woman from Samaria, Queen of the Jews, Queen of a desert that Rome had no interest in, brought back to Rome with such respect ... How could they not guess the scandal of passion ..."

"All of Rome devoured the news of that love. Every evening, every night. The slightest bit of news ... The color of her robes, the color of her eyes behind the prison windows. Her tears, the sound of her sobbing."

"Is that love greater than history says?"

"Greater, yes. You knew that?"

"Yes. Greater than he would have wished, he, the destroyer of the Temple."

"Yes, greater. Less known, too. But hold on ... I believe he didn't know he loved her. From the moment he was denied that right, he didn't believe it, you understand ... I remember that, something like that, his ignorance of his own love."

"Except perhaps when he had her at his mercy in the palace chambers, once the guards were asleep. Toward the end of night, they say."

"Yes, except perhaps then … No one knows."

Long pause. He says:

"According to you, did the people of the moor get wind of the Romans' attempt to reign over the world of thought and bodies?"

"I suppose they knew of it."

"They knew everything in those moors, those first lands to emerge from the sea."

"Yes, that's right, everything. In those subterranean moors, they knew from those who had fled the Empire, from deserters, wanderers of God, thieves. They knew all about Rome's attempt and they watched the dilapidation of its soul. And while Rome declaimed its power, you see, while it lost the blood of its very thought, the people of the holes remained plunged in the darkness of the mind."

"Thinking. Did they know what they were doing?"

"No. They didn't know how to write, or how to read. This went on for a long time, for centuries. They didn't know the meaning of those words. But I haven't told you the most important thing: their sole occupation was centered on God. With empty hands, they looked outside. At the summers. The winters. The sky. The sea. And the wind."

"That's how they acted with God. They spoke to God the way children play."

"Did you talk about a contemporary love, in your film?"

"I don't remember. It seems to me I spoke about a living love, but only about that."

"How would Rome have been involved?"

"From the very fact that the dialogue took place in Rome. These dialogues concern a love that covered Rome for centuries with a sheet of freshness. It is where the massive corpse of its history lay that the lovers could finally weep over their own history, over their love."

"What would they have wept for?"

"For themselves. Reunited by their very separation, they would finally have wept."

"You're talking about the lovers of the Temple."

"No doubt. Yes. I don't know who I'm talking about. I'm also talking about them, yes."

A pause. Silence. They are no longer looking at each other. And then he says:

"Not a word has remained of the lovers of the Temple, not a confidence, not an image, isn't that right…"

"She did not speak Roman. He did not speak the language of Samaria. It was in that hell of silence that desire grew. He was the sovereign. Irrevocable.

"And then he passed away."

"They say it was a cruel, bestial love."

"Yes, I believe it was that, a cruel, bestial love. I believe it as if it were love itself."

A pause.

"The Senate gathers its information and he takes it from there, he, the Roman chief, forced to tell her of his decision to abandon her."

"He's the one who announces it to her."

"Yes. It's evening. It happens very fast. He comes into her chambers and with incredible brutality he tells her that the boat will soon come.

"In a few days, he tells her, she will be brought to Caesarea.

"He says he can do nothing else but give her back her freedom.

"They say he cried.

"For her to live, he also tells her, she must go far away from him.

"He also says that he will never see her again."

"She does not speak Roman."

"No. But she can see he is crying. She cries because he is crying. Why she is crying, he does not know."

A pause.

"She was to die. But no. She will live a while longer."

"She lives. She does not die. She dies later, from the deception of being at once a man's captive and his lover.

"But because of this, she also lives on until the end of time.

"She lives from knowing that love is still there, whole if shattered; that it is suffering at every moment and yet still there, present, whole, and ever stronger.

"And she dies from it."

"She's crying."

"Yes, she's crying. At first she thinks she's crying for her plundered realm, for the terrifying void that awaits her. She remains alive because she is crying. She feeds on her tears. It's with a knowledge blinded by tears that she claims to love the man from Rome."

"Could his capture of her have been the cause of her passion for him?"

"Yes. Or rather, I'd say: the discovery of the violent charm of belonging to him."

"Do you think that if *he* had been captured by *her* armies, he would have been able to love her as passionately?"

"I don't believe so. No."

Look at her.
Her.
Close your eyes.
You can see that abandonment.

"Yes. I see it."

A pause. She says:

"She gives herself up to the fate offered her. She very much wants to be a queen. She very much wants to be a captive. It depends on what he desires her to be."

"Where does that genius buried within her come from?"

"Perhaps from her royal duties. And perhaps from an aptitude she has, like the women in the Gospel, those of the valleys of Jerusalem, to foresee death."

"How could he have been so unaware of her despair ..."

"Because he brought it about, I believe. You know, he believes there is nothing he can't use in the name of his kingdom."

Silence. He says:

"Behind him, since the beginning, there has been the black guard."

"Yes. He doesn't see it. He no longer sees anything. He cannot see the story he is living.

"What remains in him of the black moor is erased forever when he leaves the bedchamber."

"The black moor."

"Yes."

"Where was it … ?"

"Everywhere, I believe, in the coastal plains of the farthest lands of the North."

"Does he suffer?"

"He doesn't weep. No one knows. No. At night he cries out, at night, as when he was a child and afraid."

"Please, at least grant him some pain."

"Often the pain is unbearable when he awakens at night, knowing she is still there, and still for so short a time."

"The time that separates them from the coming of the boat that must take her to Caesarea."

"At that moment in the story, we see only the interminable reiteration of the prince's sentence: One day, one morning, a boat will come to bring you to Caesarea, your domain. Caesarea."

Silence.

MARGUERITE DURAS

"It's afterward, at that moment in the story, that I clearly see him leaving the bedchamber, stricken by death."

"And after that?"

"After that I see nothing more."

Silence.

We could have spoken, you and I, of what happened afterward, when he told her the boat was coming to take her away. We could also have spoken of what would have happened if the Senate hadn't banished her, how she would have died, alone, on a straw mat in a wing of the Roman palace, one particular night.

We could also have spoken of that interminable death, and also of that love in Caesarea, when he found her. She is twenty years old. He carries her off to marry her. Forever. He doesn't know that it's to kill her; to marry her, he says; he doesn't yet know that it's to kill her.

We could also have spoken of the discovery centuries later, in the dust of the Roman ruins, of a woman's skeleton. The bone structure told who it was. And when it had been found, and where.

How can we avoid seeing her, her, seeing *her*, that queen who is still so young? Two thousand years later.

Tall. In death, she is still tall.

Yes. Her breasts are erect. They are beautiful. They are naked beneath her prison gown.

Her legs. Her feet. Her walk. The slight swaying throughout her entire body ... Do you remember ...

A pause.

Her body must have passed through deserts, wars, the heat of Rome and the deserts, the stench of galleys, of exile. And after that we know nothing.

She is still tall. She is high. Slim. She has become lean, thin as death itself. Her hair is the black of a black bird. The green of her eyes blends with the black of the Eastern dust.

Are her eyes already drowned by death ...

No, her eyes are still drowned in the tears of her now ancient youth.

The skin of her body has separated from her body, her skeleton.

Her skin is dark, transparent, fine like silk, fragile. She has become like the silt around the springs.

Dead, she again becomes the Queen of Caesarea.
That ordinary woman, the Queen of Samaria.

The lights go off in the hotel lobby. Outside the darkness has deepened.

The fountains in the Piazza Navona have stopped flowing.

The man said that he had loved her from the moment he saw her reclining on the hotel terrace.

MARGUERITE DURAS

And then daylight comes.

He also said that she had fallen asleep in front of him and that he had been afraid, that it was then that he'd moved away from her because of the indeterminate fear spreading over his body and his eyes.

The Pure Number

č

For a long time the word "pure" was coopted by the cooking oils trade. For a long time olive oil was guaranteed pure, but never other oils, like peanut or walnut.

This word functions only when alone. In itself, by its very nature, it qualifies nothing and no one. I mean that it cannot be adapted, that it is defined in total clarity only from the moment of its use.

This word is neither a concept, nor a fault, nor a vice, nor a quality. It is a word of solitude. It is a word alone, yes, that's right, a very short word, monosyllabic. Alone. It is no doubt the "purest" of all words, beside which and after which its equivalents are erased forever, and from then on they are displaced, disoriented, floating.

I've forgotten to say that it is a sacred word in every society, in every language, in every responsibility. The world over, that's how it is with this word.

The moment Christ was born, it must have been uttered somewhere and forever. It must have been said by a passer-by, on the road, in Samaria, or by one of the women delivering the Virgin… We know nothing. Somewhere and forever this word remained, until the crucifixion of Jesus. I am not a believer. I believe only in the earthly existence of Jesus Christ. I believe that was true. That Christ and Joan of Arc must have existed: their martyrdom until the moment of death. That existed, too. These words still exist the world over.

I who do not pray, I say it, and some evenings I weep to get beyond the obligatory present—past a television of commercials, now oriented toward the future of yogurts and automobiles.

Those two, Christ and Joan of Arc, said the truth about what they thought they heard: the voice of Heaven. He, Christ, was assassinated like a political deportee. And she, Michelet's sorceress of the forests, must have been disemboweled, burned alive. Raped. Assassinated.

And already, very early in history, far off, there were Jews, the population of dead Jews, assassinated and still buried in the German soil of today; those still in the first state of consciousness choked off by death. It is still impossible to confront this event without screaming. It remains inconceivable. Germany, at the place of that assassination, has become an endemic, latent death. It has not yet awoken, so I believe. It will perhaps never again be entirely present. No doubt it is afraid of itself, of its own future, its own face. Germany is afraid of being German. They have said: Stalin. I say: Stalin, whatever he is, won the war against them, against the Nazis. Without Stalin, the Nazis would have assassinated every Jew in Europe. Without him, we would have had to kill the Germans who assassinated the Jews, do it ourselves, what *they* did, the Germans, do it to them, with them.

The word *Jew* is "pure" everywhere, but when it is said in truth we recognize it as the only word that can express what we expect from it. And what we expect from it we no longer know, because the Jewish past was incinerated by the Germans.

The "purity" of German blood was Germany's downfall. That same purity caused the assassination of millions of Jews. In Germany, and I completely believe this, this word should be publicly burned, assassinated; it should bleed only with German blood, not symbolically collected, and people should genuinely weep to see this ridiculed blood—not on themselves, but on that very blood should they weep. And this would still not be enough. Perhaps we will never know what would have been enough for this

German past to stop evolving in our lives. We will never know, perhaps.

I would like to ask the people reading these lines to help me with a project I've had for three years, since they announced the closing of the Renault factories in Billancourt. It would be to record the first and last names of all the women and all the men who spent their entire lives in that national, world-renowned factory. Since the beginning of the century, since the founding of the Renault factories in Boulogne-Billancourt.

It would be an exhaustive list, with no commentary whatsoever.

We should reach a figure the size of a large capital holding. No text could counterbalance the fact of that number, of working for Renault, the total punishment, life.

Why should we do what I'm asking?

To see what that would make in all, a wall full of proletariat.

Here, history would be that number: the truth is that number.

The proletariat in the most obvious innocence, that of the number.

The truth would be the as yet uncompared, incomparable figure of the number, the pure figure, with no commentary whatsoever, the word.

The Painting Exhibition

ℭ

for Roberto Plate

THE SPACE IS LARGE. At the top of a wall, windows. The sky is still and blue. Only one thick cloud leaves the blue. Very slowly, it moves beyond the windows, the blueness.

There are no books. There are no words printed on a newspaper. There is no vocabulary in a dictionary. Everything is perfectly in order.

In the middle of the space is a low table, beneath which is another, lower table. The two tables are covered with empty tubes of paint, bent, often cut in the middle, often cut and spread open, scraped clean with knife blades.

The open tubes and those still intact are not mixed in with the disemboweled, emptied ones. They are round, full, very healthy, very firm, like fruits that have not quite reached maturity. They have been placed so that the labels telling their colors can't be seen. Altogether they form a supple grey metallic alloy. Under their caps, they are hermetically sealed.

In a jar on that same table are some brushes. There are fifty brushes, maybe even one hundred. They all seem practically destroyed. They have been reduced; they are crushed, flared out, hairless; all are stiff with dried paint, and comical, too. They do not have the tangibility of the paint in the tubes, nor of the man speaking. You might think they'd been found in a cavern, in a tomb along the Nile.

In the midst of that conglomeration of objects, there is a man. He is alone. He is wearing a white shirt and blue jeans. He is speaking. He points to several cubic feet of paintings, lined up against another wall. He says they are the ones that have been painted, the ones for the exhibition.

There are many of them. They are all turned toward the wall. All the paint missing from the tubes went onto those canvases. That is where it now is, on the canvases whose progress it halted.

The man speaks. He says the paintings are not all the same size. We might take him at his word, but no, they are of different formats. That difference, different each time, poses a mysterious problem for the man. Sometimes one can mix large paintings with small paintings. This time, it isn't possible. He doesn't know why, but he knows he must explain this.

He speaks alone, aloud; sometimes his voice quickens and shouts. We do not know if he shouts while paintings are being made. We know that they are always being made, day and night, while this man sleeps or while he is awake.

The man speaks in an idiosyncratic French. Everything he says, he says in this French that only he speaks. He stopped progressing in this language. It took up his time and it wasn't worth it.

He talks about hanging his paintings. He will do it himself. He talks about that. He says where, in what part of the city, the exhibition will take place: near the Seine, in a former book-binding studio.

The man says he hasn't shown his paintings in seven years. He has another job in life, which he takes great pleasure in, that isn't the issue. The desire to show his work suddenly returned to him very strongly, before the spring. He says: Seven years, it's just that I'm starting over, I think, no?

He speaks more and more quickly; he apologizes; he says it's because he's nervous. Seven years. He says: I stopped altogether. I shut myself up in here for four months. At the end of four months the exhibition was ready. He says that what counts is determination.

Eventually he gets where he had to.
He begins to show the paintings for the Exhibition.

One by one he picks them up, and when he reaches the wall opposite the one they were leaning against he turns them around. Whether he's carrying them or turning them around, he keeps talking. At times he seems almost hesitant to turn them around; then he does it, he turns them.

He is still speaking about an order he'd like to observe in the exhibition. He doesn't want any one painting to be highlighted at another's expense. He'd like a natural order that would put all the paintings on an equal footing on the walls of the exhibition. In no case should the canvases be isolated, dominant, or else lost. They must be together, must almost touch each other, almost—yes, that's right. They must not be separated the way they are here, you understand?

In bursts, canvas by canvas, the paintings come to light.

The man says these paintings are of the same person, made at the same moment in that person's life. That is why he wants to hang them all together; he is quite preoccupied by this. He is not saying he wants them all to be one, no, that's not it at all, not at all; but they should hang next to each other in a true and natural juxtaposition, for which he alone is responsible, whose value he alone should know.

He talks a lot about the distance between the canvases. He says that sometimes there should be almost none. And sometimes perhaps none at all, that they should butt against each other, yes, sometimes. He doesn't know, really. He is in the same state as we are before these paintings he made, overwrought.

The man reveals his paintings while maintaining a continuous flow of speech. He speaks so that his words will sound while the paintings enter into the light. He speaks so that a discomfort will arise, so that deliverance from pain will finally occur.

In the end, we leave him alone to get on with his drudgery. We leave him to his misfortune, to that infernal obligation that outstrips any commentary, any metaphor, any ambiguity. In other words, we leave him to his own story. We have entered into the violence of the paintings he made. We look at them; we do not look at him, the man speaking, the painter, the man struggling in the continent of silence. We look at them, at them alone. The man speaking is the one who made them without knowing what he was doing, outside of meaning, in a profound distraction.

One can always say that all paintings move at the same speed. Sometimes they pass on wings, as if guided. Sometimes it seems that the force leading them is shown like a wave that buries itself, with its blue-black color.

That above, when one rises toward these forces, in the sky, there might be the face of sleeping child. It's barely a child, barely a sky, nothing that can be said. Nothing. But painting in its entirety.

That a white room with a white floor crosses through, open on the void, and at a door flap a piece of white curtain has remained.

That there are also livestock with no identity, bloated pouches, the softness of very ancient paintings that identified them. Signs that look like things. Tree trunks that leave, go away. Sections of sea serpents in the dampness of springs, of foam. Possible cascades, surges, juxtapositions between ideas, things, the permanence of things, their inanity, the material of ideas, colors, light, and God knows what else.